Rosemary Wells

Forest of Dreams

paintings by Susan Jeffers

Dial Books for Young Readers

New York

God made me new |
Just like the spring that waits beneath the snow.

Published by
Dial Books for Young Readers
A Division of NAL Penguin Inc.
2 Park Avenue · New York, New York 10016

Published simultaneously in Canada
by Fitzhenry & Whiteside Limited, Toronto
Text copyright © 1988 by Rosemary Wells
Pictures copyright © 1988 by Susan Jeffers
All rights reserved · Printed in the U.S.A.
Design by Atha Tehon
First Edition
(a)

Library of Congress Cataloging in Publication Data
Wells, Rosemary. Forest of dreams.
Summary: A child praises God for the beauty of nature.
[1. Nature—Fiction. 2. Stories in rhyme.]
I. Jeffers, Susan, ill. II. Title.
PZ8.3.W465Fo 1988   [E]   88-3826
ISBN 0-8037-0569-7
ISBN 0-8037-0570-0 (lib. bdg.)

The art for each picture consists of an oil painting,
which is color-separated and reproduced in full color.

God made me small
Just like the fawn that sleeps inside the doe.

God gave me eyes
To see the woods and all who live within it.
To watch the winter sun last
Every evening one more minute.

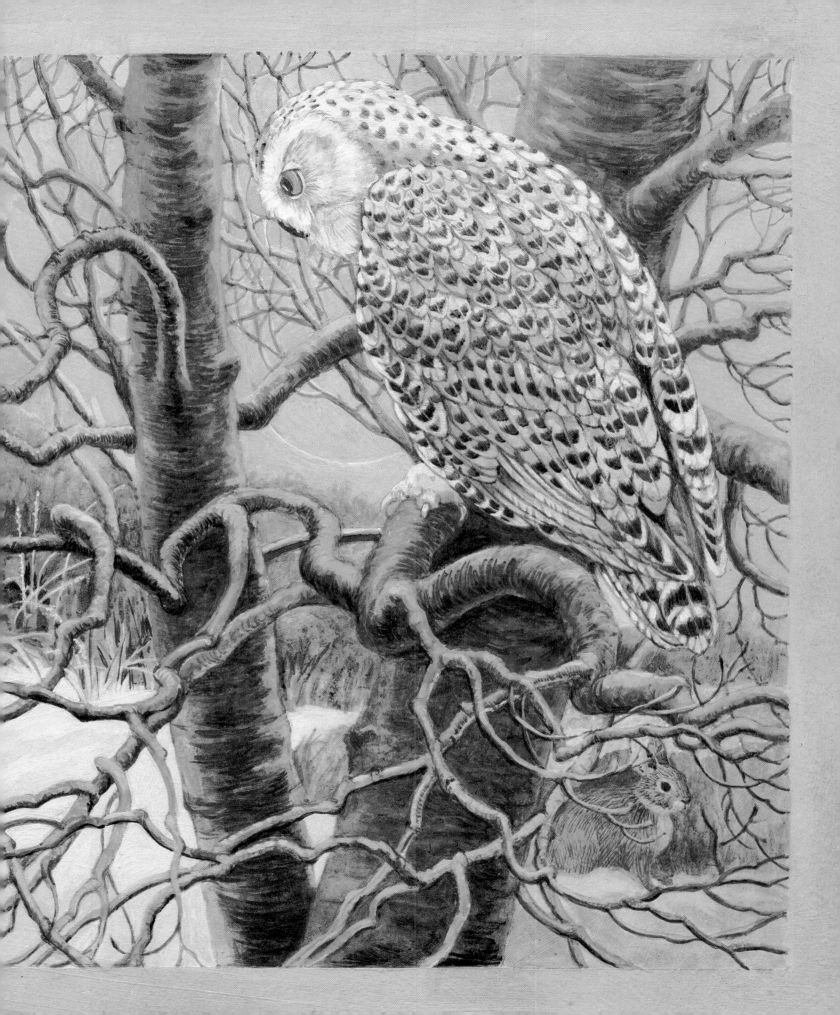

God gave me hands to touch the ice
Stiff and diamond bright,
That spills upon the pine tree
And sparkles up the night.

God gave me strength to climb the tree
Prickly, thick, and high.
I sit inside the winter wind
While all the branches sigh.

Below the frozen salt marsh
There's music in the stream.
God gave me ears to hear it whisper
Like a summer's dream.

God lets me feel
The morning rain, sifting, drifting down.
And I can smell the sunlight burrow
Softly underground.

The earth begins to open
A sparrow starts to sing,

God gave me time to listen.
God gave me everything.